SHORT TALES
Greek Myths

ACHILLES

Adapted by Christopher E. Long
Illustrated by Brian Churilla

GREEN LEVEL
- Familiar topics
- Frequently used words
- Repeating language patterns

BLUE LEVEL
- New ideas introduced
- Larger vocabulary
- Variety of language patterns

PINK LEVEL
- More complex ideas
- Extended vocabulary
- Expanded sentence structures

To learn more about Short Tales leveling, go to www.abdopublishing.com

Published by Magic Wagon, a division of the ABDO Publishing Group, 8000 West 78th Street, Edina, Minnesota, 55439. Copyright © 2008 by Abdo Consulting Group, Inc. International copyrights reserved in all countries. All rights reserved. No part of this book may be reproduced in any form without written permission from the publisher. Short Tales ™ is a trademark and logo of Magic Wagon.

Printed in the United States.

Adapted Text by Christopher E. Long
Illustrations by Brian Churilla
Colors by Jeremy Shepherd
Edited by Stephanie Hedlund
Interior Layout by Kristen Fitzner Denton
Book Design and Packaging by Shannon Eric Denton

Library of Congress Cataloging-in-Publication Data
Long, Christopher E.
  Achilles / adapted by Christopher E. Long ; illustrated by Brian Churilla.
     p. cm. -- (Short tales. Greek myths)
  ISBN 978-1-60270-133-5
  1. Achilles (Greek mythology)--Juvenile literature. I. Churilla, Brian. II. Title.
BL820.A22L66 2008
398.20938'02--dc22

                                        2007036062

THE GREEK GODS

ZEUS:
Ruler of Gods
& Men

ATHENA:
Goddess of
Wisdom

HEPHAESTUS:
God of Fire
& Metalworking

HERA:
Goddess of Marriage
Queen of the Gods

HERMES:
Messenger of
the Gods

HESTIA:
Goddess of the
Hearth & Home

POSEIDON:
God of the Sea

APHRODITE:
Goddess of Love

ARES:
God of War

ARTEMIS:
Goddess of
the Hunt

APOLLO:
God of the Sun

HADES:
God of the
Underworld

MYTHICAL BEGINNING

Zeus was the supreme ruler of the gods. He fell in love with Thetis, a sea nymph. Thetis's beauty captured the hearts and minds of all who saw her. But Themis, the goddess of law and justice, had a vision about Thetis. Themis said that Thetis would have a son who would be more powerful than his father.

Zeus did not want anyone to be more powerful than him. So, he decided not to take Thetis as his wife. Instead, he arranged for Thetis to marry Peleus.

A year after the wedding, Thetis gave birth to Achilles. Thetis wanted to protect her son from all harm. So, she traveled to the river Styx. It flowed between Earth and the Underworld. She knew all areas of the human body touched by the water would be protected.

Thetis stood on the bank of the river Styx clutching her baby son.

"Achilles, my only son," she said, "once your body is touched by the water you won't ever be hurt."

She removed the blanket wrapped around her child.

Thetis held Achilles by the heel.

She quickly lowered him into the river.

Soon, Achilles was completely under the water except for the heel that his mother held.

Even though he was a baby, Achilles was not frightened.

He felt the magical waters wash over him.

Moments later, Thetis pulled Achilles out of the river.

She dried him off with the blanket. She never noticed the water hadn't touched his heel.

Achilles grew to be a strong, handsome young man.

The best soldiers in Sparta trained him to be a great warrior.

Achilles and his best friend, Patroclus, worked hard to master the art of combat.

They trained all day, every day.

Patroclus was a better warrior than most of the other boys.

But Achilles was the best of all.

Even before he reached manhood, Achilles could outdo his adult teachers.

People said that Ares, the god of war, favored Achilles over everyone.

"Achilles, it doesn't matter how hard I train," Patroclus said. "I will never be as good a warrior as you."

"I get cuts and bruises," Patroclus said, "but you never get a single scratch."

Achilles wrapped his arm around his friend's shoulder and smiled.

"Then I promise that I will always be there to protect you from harm," Achilles said.

When Achilles and Patroclus reached manhood, Sparta waged war on Troy.

Achilles was excited that he would finally be able to go into battle.

He was eager to test his skills against the legendary Trojan soldiers.

Patroclus and Achilles boarded a ship to set sail for Troy.

A thousand Spartan ships sailed across the sea.

Nearly all the Spartan soldiers had heard of Achilles.

His reputation as the best fighter in Sparta circulated throughout the army.

"But let's see how Achilles is in actual battle," some of the soldiers said.

As the fleet of Spartan ships approached the shore, Achilles turned to Patroclus.

"Stay near me when the battle begins," Achilles said. "I'll make sure that you aren't hurt."

"Don't worry about me, Achilles," Patroclus grinned. "I'll be just fine."

When the battle began, the Spartan soldiers watched
Achilles in wide-eyed wonder.

He showed his fellow Spartans that the stories of him
being the greatest warrior were true.

Achilles fought 15 Trojan soldiers at the same time.

He drove them back as if he were the god of war himself.

The Trojan soldiers tried everything to beat Achilles.

Fire arrows bounced off him as if he were made of stone.

Trojan swords shattered when they struck him.

Achilles stormed through the Trojans as if they weren't there at all.

Soon, Achilles found himself surrounded by 50 Trojans.

The Trojans raised their swords and attacked Achilles.

Achilles, holding a sword in each hand, defended himself with ease.

The Trojans ran away from Achilles. They knew they could not beat him.

The Spartan soldiers cheered as they watched the Trojan soldiers retreat.

"The gods have blessed you, Achilles!" the Spartans cheered.

Achilles looked around for Patroclus.

During the battle, Achilles had lost sight of his friend.

"Has anyone seen Patroclus?" Achilles shouted.

A nearby Spartan soldier pointed to a body on the beach.

Achilles rushed over and found his friend wounded.

"Patroclus, I'm so sorry that I failed you," Achilles said.

Patroclus looked up at Achilles.

"Achilles, you haven't failed me," Patroclus said.

"Who did this to you?" Achilles asked his friend.

Patroclus weakly replied, "It was Prince Hector of Troy."

"I swear to Zeus that I will avenge you." Achilles said.

Achilles watched helplessly as his friend slowly slipped away.

By the light of the moon, Achilles buried Patroclus.

The only thing on Achilles's mind was finding Prince Hector of Troy.

Achilles marched away from the Spartans' camp.

"Achilles, where are you going?" a general asked.

"To hunt down Prince Hector," Achilles answered.

"Wait until morning," the general said. "We'll invade Troy then."

But Achilles didn't listen.

He decided to find Prince Hector by himself.

After all, he owed it to Patroclus.

The Spartan soldiers watched as their greatest warrior walked alone toward Troy.

Achilles walked through the night. He reached the palace of Troy at daybreak.

Achilles stood outside the gate with a sword in each hand.

"Prince Hector of Troy," he yelled, "come out and face me!"

Surrounded by Trojan soldiers, Prince Hector peered down from the palace wall.

"You're just one man," Prince Hector laughed. "What have I done to make you do such a stupid thing?"

"You killed Patroclus!" Achilles shouted.

"Perhaps," Prince Hector said. "Who was he?"

Through clenched teeth, Achilles said, "He was my friend."

Achilles watched as the palace's gate opened.

Prince Hector led the Trojan army out to Achilles.

The Trojans surrounded Achilles.

"Who are you, Spartan?" Prince Hector asked.

"I am Achilles," he answered.

A murmur spread throughout the Trojan army.

"I have heard of you," Prince Hector said. "It will be an honor to do battle with you."

Achilles and Prince Hector were soon locked in combat.

The noise from the battle reached Mount Olympus.

Zeus and the other gods watched the fight.

It was a battle for the ages.

Both men fought bravely.

But Prince Hector was no match for Achilles.

Before Achilles could finish the battle, Zeus removed Prince Hector's body from the battlefield.

Zeus whispered in Achilles's ear, "You won, Achilles. But Prince Hector fought valiantly."

"He deserves to pass on to the next world as a true warrior," Zeus said.

Prince Paris was Hector's younger brother. He was overcome with grief by his brother's passing.

He aimed his bow and arrow at Achilles.

"Save your arrow, Trojan," Achilles said. "It will not harm me."

In utter defeat, Prince Paris dropped his bow.

Upon falling, the arrow fired along the ground.

It skipped across the dirt toward Achilles's foot.

The arrow lodged into Achilles's heel.

Suddenly, Achilles fell to the ground.

After so many others had failed, Achilles was defeated with a single arrow!

It had struck the only spot that was not protected.

This heel had not been touched by the waters of the Styx.

The gods on Mount Olympus wept for Achilles.

He had stood before the Trojan army carrying only his swords and bravery.

So, the gods made a vow on that day.

Achilles's name would be remembered forever.